Hello, Family Members,

Learning to read is one of the most  s of early childhood. **Hello Reader!** p children become skilled readers w g readers learn to read by remembering frequently used ds like "the," "is," and "and"; by using phonics skills to decode new words; and by interpreting picture and text clues. These books provide both the stories children enjoy and the structure they need to read fluently and independently. Here are suggestions for helping your child *before*, *during*, and *after* reading:

Before

- Look at the cover and pictures and have your child predict what the story is about.
- Read the story to your child.
- Encourage your child to chime in with familiar words and phrases.
- Echo read with your child by reading a line first and having your child read it after you do.

During

- Have your child think about a word he or she does not recognize right away. Provide hints such as "Let's see if we know the sounds" and "Have we read other words like this one?"
- Encourage your child to use phonics skills to sound out new words.
- Provide the word for your child when more assistance is needed so that he or she does not struggle and the experience of reading with you is a positive one.
- Encourage your child to have fun by reading with a lot of expression . . . like an actor!

After

- Have your child keep lists of interesting and favorite words.
- Encourage your child to read the books over and over again. Have him or her read to brothers, sisters, grandparents, and even teddy bears. Repeated readings develop confidence in young readers.
- Talk about the stories. Ask and answer questions. Share ideas about the funniest and most interesting characters and events in the stories.

I do hope that you and your child enjoy this book.

—Francie Alexander
Reading Specialist,
Scholastic's Learning Ventures

To my wife Cindy and my children,
Emma and Daniel ... you keep my motor running!
— B.B.

TONKA® and TONKA JOE® are trademarks of Hasbro, Inc.
Copyright © 2001 Hasbro, Inc.
All rights reserved. Published by Scholastic Inc.
SCHOLASTIC, HELLO READER, CARTWHEEL BOOKS and associated logos
are trademarks and/or registered trademarks of Scholastic Inc.

Library of Congress Cataloging-in-Publication Data

Herman, Gail,
     Meet Tonka Joe / by Gail Herman ; illustrated by Bob Berry.
          p.   cm.— (Hello reader! Level 2)
     Summary: Tonka Joe makes sure his various vehicles, including
the Pulverizer, Flame Racer, Blizzard Rig, and Hazard Handler, are
ready for any emergency.
     ISBN 0-439-25730-1 (pbk.)
     [1. Emergency vehicles—Fiction.] I. Berry, Bob- ill. II. Title. III.
Series.
PZ7.H4315 Me 2001
[E]—dc21

                                                                                 00-061247

12 11 10 9 8 7 6 5 4 3 2   01 02 03 04 05

Printed in the U.S.A.   24
First printing, May 2001

Meet Tonka Joe

by Gail Herman
Illustrated by Bob Berry

Hello Reader! —Level 2

SCHOLASTIC INC. Cartwheel B·O·O·K·S®

New York   Toronto   London   Auckland   Sydney
Mexico City   New Delhi   Hong Kong

Hello! My name is Tonka Joe, and this is where I live — Minnetonka!

There are lots of exciting
places here —
the fireworks factory...
the raceway where my trucks
go wild...
and the mountain that is really
a volcano.

This is the street corner where I see
my niece J.J. and my nephew Stevie!
"Hi, Uncle Joe!" says J.J.
"Want to come and play with us?"
asks Stevie.
"That would be nice," I answer.

Then I pat the Pulverizer.
"But this truck is giving me
a bumpy ride.
I have to check it
at my workshop."

At the shop,
I strap on my tool belt.
I twist here,
turn there.

The jackhammer has to smash boulders and smash them fast— just like it did when a rock slide hit. The town would have been buried....

But I roared into action with the
Pulverizer.
The truck crashed through rocks.
Its jackhammer broke boulders
to bits.
It stopped the slide!

There! The Pulverizer is tuned up
and ready to go.
But it is important to keep all
my trucks in tip-top shape.

You never know when
disaster could strike....

Once there was a fire
at the fireworks factory.
Explosions! Fire balls!
Fire trucks couldn't stop the blaze.
So I jumped into my
Flame Racer and sped to
the scene with sonic speed.

I let loose with the power hose.
Water blasted the flames.
In seconds, they sputtered out.
Now that's power!

All right, the Flame Racer is
in shape.
What about the Blizzard Rig?

Once, a mighty snowstorm
trapped children in the school....

Until the Blizzard Rig roared
into action!
Its super-strong shovels
dug out mounds of snow.

We plowed through the storm,
one, two, three.
Hooray! What a rescue!

Okay, the Blizzard Rig is set to go.
Now let's check the FireWalker—
a mega-truck for
a mega-emergency!
I remember when a skyscraper
went up....

Disaster struck!
Glass flew through the air.
Beams hurled to the ground.
One worker hung onto a platform.

"I'll save you!" I cried.
Up, up, up I went!
In no time at all,
the worker was safe on the ground.

Now the FireWalker is ready.
What next?
Beep! Beep!
Uh-oh! A message on the computer!

It's from J.J. and Stevie.
"Come to the mountain!"
It must be an emergency.
Is the volcano erupting?
Is there an earthquake?
A forest fire?

I'll take the Hazard Handler.
It's great for any emergency!
I zoom through town,
then up the mountain path.

There they are!
"What's wrong?" I shout.
"Nothing!" says Stevie.

J.J. points to a picnic basket.
"We did not mean to scare you,"
she says.
"It's not an emergency.
We want to have a picnic —
with you!"

I am happy Stevie and J.J. are safe, and I am happy to spend time with them, too.
"I'm hungry!" I say.
"Let's eat!"